To Yoko

First published in Great Britain by Andersen Press Ltd., 2009

Printed and bound in Singapore

First American edition, 2009

1 3 5 7 9 10 8 6 4 2

www.fsgkidsbooks.com

Library of Congress Cataloging-in-Publication Data is available upon request.

David Lucas

Cake Girl

FARRAR, STRAUS AND GIROUX

NEW YORK

The Witch was alone
on her birthday . . . *again!*

So she baked
a Cake Girl.

And told her to sing
"Happy Birthday."

And dance.

And smile.

And make her laugh.

And do all the housework . . .

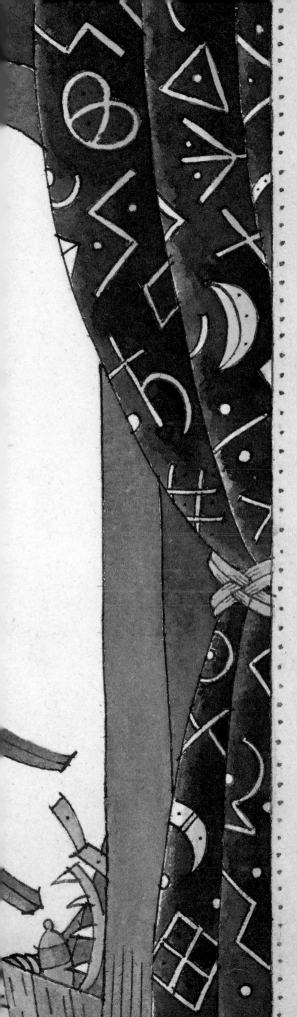

"And then," said the Witch,
"I'll eat you."

HAPPY BIRTHDAY TO ME

What shall I do?
wondered Cake Girl.

She looked up.
"I expect you're having
a big birthday party?"
she said.

"Party?"
said the Witch.
"I'm not having a party."

Her hat spun around
and she turned away.

"No one likes me," she said.

"But why don't you use MAGIC
to make people like you?" said Cake Girl.

"I made you," said the Witch,
"and you don't like me."

"But you're not nice to me,"
said Cake Girl.

"Hmmm . . ."
The Witch was thinking.
Her hat spun around at great speed.

"Do you mean that
if I was nice to you,
then you'd like me?"

"Yes," said Cake Girl.
"Promise?" said the Witch.
"Yes," said Cake Girl.

"But I don't know
how to be nice,"
said the Witch.

"Perhaps you could help me?" said Cake Girl.
"Oh yes! That's easy!" said the Witch, and snapped her fingers—
the housework was done in a flash.

"And perhaps . . ."
said Cake Girl,
a little nervously,

"you don't have
to eat me?"

"*Hmmm . . .*" said the Witch.

"Difficult. You *do* look delicious . . ."

She stroked her chin.

"Well, I suppose I could have a
bit of bread and butter instead."

"And perhaps," said Cake Girl, feeling braver now,
"you could sing *me* a song?"
"Oho!" said the Witch. "Me? Sing?"

She did her best.

"And dance!" said Cake Girl, happily.

"And smile!"

"And make me laugh!"

"And do MAGIC tricks!"
said Cake Girl,
clapping her soft
marzipan hands.

"Oh, I love doing magic tricks!"
said the Witch.

And she turned herself
into a great big fancy cake—
and laughed and laughed
until she nearly crumbled to bits.

"I can turn myself into
anything!" she said.

"And you too, if you like!" said the Witch. "I can turn you into anything. Anything at all!"

"A princess!" said Cake Girl. And suddenly she was a princess, and the Witch was a splendidly wicked-looking queen.

"Or a firework!" said Cake Girl—
and they shot into the sky
with a bang.

They fluttered back down as birds.

And then the Witch showed Cake Girl
(who wasn't made of cake anymore)
how to work magic
and turn herself into
whatever she liked.

And when they were tired,
the Witch turned into
a big comfortable armchair
and Cake Girl turned into a cat.

They couldn't have wished
for a more magical birthday.